BRIDGE 6

Jim McGugan

Judith Christine Mills

Stoddart
Kids
TORONTO • NEW YORK

*We acknowledge the Canada Council for the Arts and the
Ontario Arts Council for their support of our publishing program.*

Published in Canada in 1999 by Stoddart Kids,
a division of Stoddart Publishing Co. Limited
34 Lesmill Road
Toronto, ON M3B 2T6
Tel (416) 445-3333 Fax (416) 445-5967
E-mail Customer.Service@ccmailgw.genpub.com

Distributed in Canada by
General Distribution Services
325 Humber College Blvd.,
Toronto, ON M9W 7C3
Tel (416) 213-1919 Fax (416) 213-1917
E-mail Customer.Service@ccmailgw.genpub.com

Published in the United States in 1999 by Stoddart Kids,
a division of Stoddart Publishing Co. Limited
180 Varick Street, 9th Floor
New York, New York 14207
Toll free 1-800-805-1083
E-mail gdsinc@genpub.com

Distributed in the United States by
General Distribution Services
85 River Rock Drive, Suite 202
Buffalo, New York 14207
Toll free 1-800-805-1083
E-mail gdsinc@genpub.com

Canadian Cataloguing in Publication Data

McGugan, Jim, 1948–
Bridge 6

ISBN 0-7737-3137-7

I. Mills, Judith. II. Title. III. Title: Bridge six.

PS8575.G853B74 1999   jC813'.54   C98-931788-9
PZ7.M478Br 1999

A weekly hockey game is the scene of an escalating
power struggle between a young girl's two older brothers.
Afraid her family is coming apart, she cleverly thinks
of a way for everyone to win.

Printed in Hong Kong

For Sis and Alex.
— J.M.

For my husband, Robert Horton, with love.
— J.C.M.

Those winter mornings at our truck stop diner were heated with Owen's rules. My older brother would smack his skillet with a wooden spoon and holler at folks. "Use a fork. Wipe your hands. Finish them beans!" Owen loved rules, hockey, and cooking.

Drivers used to scrap like grizzly bears reaching for Owen's *Crème Caramel* until he made another rule: no jabbing, socking or clobbering during jiggly desserts.

"Your brother's one fine cook, Kelly," they whispered, "but he's better at dishing out rules." I had to agree. Still, I never grumbled and we got by.

It was my other brother, Prunes, who fussed and fumed and finally quit the diner for good. Prunes hated rules. And now, he didn't have any home at all — not even a backwoods shack. Prunes slept under the Number 6 Railroad Bridge instead.

Owen didn't like that. Neither did I. Sometimes, when the midnight train howled through the valley like a sorry dog, I'd bolt awake, wondering if Prunes was warm.

I'd worry that he was wet or hurting or starving himself skinny or being bitten by a rat.

"Piff," said Prunes.

He said Bridge 6 *was* a home as much as any, and he was thankful for his soft snowy mattress, the breezes and the view. "I've found a giant's bedroom, Kelly," Prunes would say, "dressed without rules." Rules and Prunes were enemies, and now he wouldn't come home because of them. No matter what.

So we went to Prunes. Every Saturday Owen emptied the diner and taped a card in the window. *Hockey At Bridge 6*, it read. *Bring Old Sweaters And A Jar Of Potato Soup. Truckers Welcome.*

One Saturday, when the air was as cold as silver, Prunes rolled about in his blanket, growling. Prunes was a blizzard of growls. "Who's in goal?" he asked. Then he winked at me.

Prunes knew I was gawky and graceless and couldn't even skate. He suspected I might never score a goal. But he said my shot blocking and my leg kicks whipped him into such a fidget, he could barely swallow spit. He was certain I could be the greatest goalie in the family — if I ever got a chance to play.

This time Prunes rose up chilled and stiff, staring Owen in the eye. "So, who *is* going in goal, Owen? How about somebody else?"

Our customers enjoyed this part of the game. Even the truckers laughed. Every Saturday Prunes fought to make me goalie. "Stupendous idea, Prunes," they cheered.

"Not. Not. Not!" shouted Owen, holding up his goaltender pads. "I'm the oldest. The oldest is always in goal. That's the rule!"

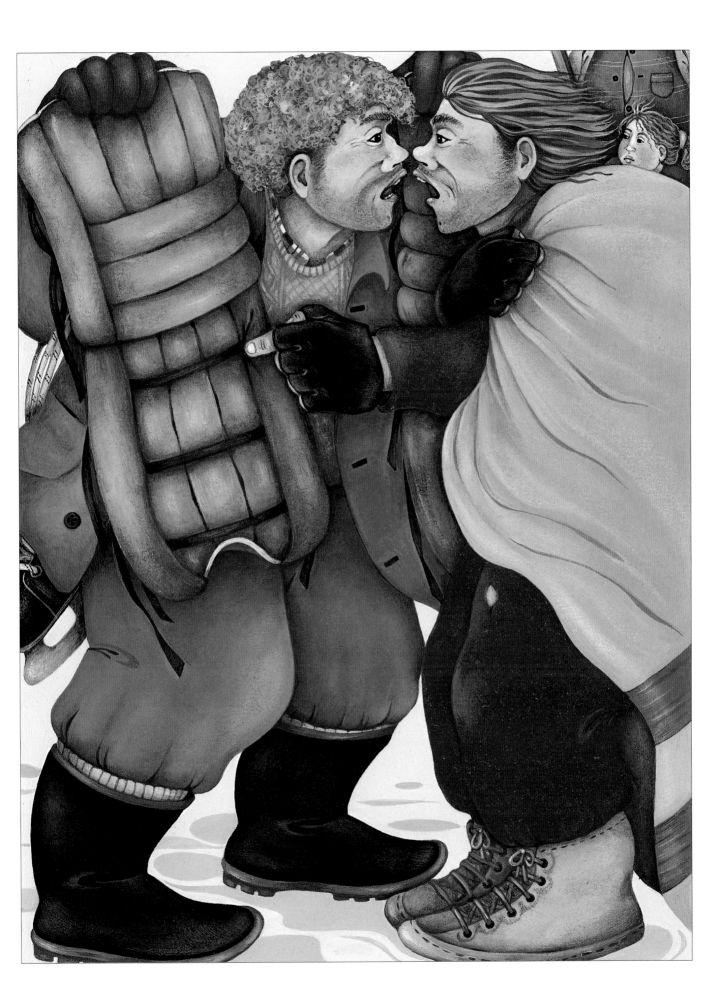

"Piff."

Prunes was extra growly that morning. He said he was starting a list of silly thinkers and printing Owen's name on top. He pulled a chewed crayon out of his pocket. "And I'm drawing a *fat* line under it." So he did.

Then, poking the paper under his cap, he charged down the bank to the sawmill pond while we swirled behind like puffs of smoke.

Prunes charged across the ice, bumping and spearing and pushing his elbows high. Prunes owned the snappiest elbows. Their tips curved into fangs that gnawed holes in his sleeves.

"Ouch," Owen moaned, rubbing his ear.

Prunes grinned and patted his hat. "Tough turnips, Owen. You're on my list." Then he signaled me and we dashed toward the net. "Be fair. Let her play goal."

Owen had rules for reading and rules for bedtime and rules for dusting nutmeg on *Butternut Squash Compote*. The oldest always chose what position to play, and Owen chose goalkeeper. He shook his head. I couldn't be goalie.

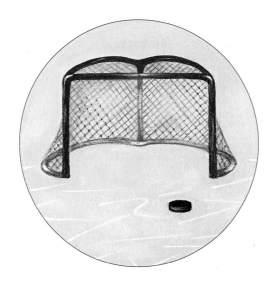

But when the game began, Owen's legs were slower than syrup. He flopped on his ankles and fumbled his stick. He could halt a falling soufflé, but hockey pucks zinged right by him into the net.

Prunes howled. "You gallumping bag of nothin', Owen. Let someone else play goal!"

"Splendid idea, Prunes," said the others.

"Not. Not. Not!" Owen shouted back.

Maybe it was the flood of potato soup, or perhaps it was only the cold, but this time Prunes was firm. "Be fair, Owen. Be fair or I won't play hockey — ever again!"

Owen's chin dropped to his collar and he held his breath for a long, long time. Finally he wimpered, "But I'm the oldest, Prunes."

"Piff. No more rules, Owen. Play fair or I'm catching the next train out of the valley. No matter what."

With my heart thumping, I scrambled forward, but tripped on a rut. "Owen!" I cried. "Prunes!"

Owen raised his head. "We need rules, Prunes." But he bent to the ice anyway, and slowly unbuckled his pads.

A hard wind flapped our pant bottoms and Prunes tightened his scarf. He watched Owen place his pads on the snowbank and angle himself like an old broom against a pine. And leaning there with his teeth a-clacking, Owen didn't look like anybody's oldest brother.

For a moment I stood icicle still, then I gave Prunes a nudge.

"I'm thinkin'," said Prunes. "And I'm thinkin' the fairest . . ."
Another stinging gust lifted Prunes' cap as easily as a feather and
plopped it at his feet. ". . . the fairest thing to do is to draw
names out of this hat. Everybody's name goes in, then Luck will
choose our goalie."

I didn't like Prunes' plan. I itched to go in goal, but I felt horribly
for Owen.

I yanked Prunes' scarf and pulled him down. I whispered in his ear, and when I quit Prunes laughed and shouted across the pond.

"Everybody's name goes in, folks. *And I'm writing the names.*"

Prunes' pockets were lumpy with bottles and lost things he'd found by the side of the road. From inside, he grabbed a fistful of papers and a short, dirty pencil, while the other skaters pushed and barked out their names. Prunes shooed them away, but when his cap was filled, he held it out. "Pick one, Kelly." Owen edged forward trying to peek.

I read the name so softly, no one heard. So I held it high for everyone to see. Then I shouted the name out twice.

"Piff!" said Prunes. But he lowered his elbows and smiled at me when the new game began.

Later at the diner, between bites of *Maple Sugar Pie*, the truck drivers said they had never seen any goaltender block shots faster or get leg kicks higher. And Prunes said it was the best hockey that goalie had ever played.

Everyone probably guessed there was only one name written on all those slips of paper. And maybe there's a rule that says every name should have been different. But Prunes hated rules.

There was only one name in that hat, of course. Owen's.

And Owen? He supposed he'd played pretty well, all right, but next Saturday he was ready to try something new.

"In case you hadn't noticed," he announced, "I like rules. If you like rules, then being referee is the right job to have."

And maybe it was.

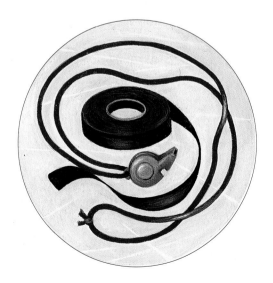